Comment by George Polley, author of 'The Old Man & The Monkey' and 'Grandfather and the Raven': The Eye of Erasmus" is a tale gently and beautifully told. Like the Harry Potter novels, it is a book that readers of all ages will enjoy. It is definitely a book that I will read again and again (I have just ordered a copy).

Comment by Christina Hall Volkoff, author of 'Travels Through Love And Time': It flows like a fairy tale; it operates on multiple levels of reality and unreality; it is a delightful fantasy that transports you into this world as if you had inhabited it already all your life.

Comment from Stacey Danson, author of 'Empty Chairs': From the mother sitting bathing her feet in the cool water thinking of the sister so wrongfully hung, we have a sense that the as yet unborn seventh child is indeed special. A marvellous book that will grab and hold its readers.

Comment from Andrew C. Wilson, author of 'The Domino Effect': *You have a knack for keeping the reader wanting more.*

Comment from Liz Hoban, author of 'The Cheech Room': *This is a compelling read that your readers will devour. My only complaint is I want more.*

To The Ashford LRC
Enjoy the read

Teresa Goering

F/GEE

The Eye of Erasmus

01/2012

F/GEE   L08778X0589

ISBN   1453634754

EAN   9781453634752

"The Eye of Erasmus" was first published by Night Publishing, a trading name of Valley Strategies Ltd., a UK-registered private limited-liability company, registration number 5796186. Night Publishing can be contacted at: http://www.nightpublishing.com.

Acknowledgements

My thanks go to the following:

Neil Minter, who without realising it encouraged me endlessly.

Richard Grayling of Struggling Authors.co.uk. Whether he likes it or not, he is my newly appointed 'PR man'. Richard picked me up every time I was crushed by rejection, and helped me on my way forward.

Richard Reg Jones because he made me laugh at rejection instead of cry.

John Piggott for the wonderful art work on the book cover.

My dearest friend Lesley Piggott for keeping me focused when I just wanted to walk away

Tim Roux, my editor, for his exceptional help in sorting out my 'fluffed' up lines.

Dedication

I lovingly dedicate this book to my son Matt, his partner Charmaine who gave birth to my beautiful granddaughter Madison Teresa.

Let the good times roll.

Chapter 1

The 30th October was a beautiful autumn day, remarkably warm for the time of year. A weak sun appeared through rain filled clouds. Agastine, heavy with an overdue child, stopped walking and supported the baby with both hands around her stomach.

For most of the morning there had been constant movement. Maybe at last she could bring this infant into the world, she thought contentedly. Gently with her right hand she caressed the child and he seemed to settle. She had borne six daughters and this time she was convinced the child was a boy.

She had carried him for nine months and everything had been different this time. It had not been an easy pregnancy and on many occasions she had taken to her bed, more by necessity than choice. Agastine had already chosen the name. Her husband had smiled at this. Whilst he was assured in himself that he would have another daughter, he gave in to his wife's whims.

Tiring now, she sat down on one of the rocks and, removing her shoes with difficulty, allowed the gentle movement of the waves to cool her feet. Her mind wandered back to summers past, growing up with her beloved sister Drendell. They were both fascinated by the seashore and spent endless days playing on these rocks when the tide was out. Sadly she was no longer around and she missed her dreadfully.

The previous year she had been hung as a witch.

Drendell had been trying to help a new baby boy who had trouble breathing. Her potions had always worked in the past but this time she was unsuccessful and the boy had died. A rejected admirer spitefully accused her of being a witch in the hearing of a couple of villagers and the word had spread and magnified.

She had been dragged from her home in the middle of the night and hanged from the oak tree in the centre of the village. Agastine, although overwrought on hearing this, rushed out to retrieve her body. With the help of a passing stranger who took pity on her, she wrapped Drendell in a sheet and took her away on an old cart she had pulled herself. In doing so she had lost the baby she was unaware had been growing inside her.

This child she was now carrying would be in memory of her beloved Drendell. Agastine loved all her children dearly but this one would be special.

With a deep sigh she struggled to put her shoes back on and pulled herself up slowly with the aid of a nearby rock. She then made her way back to the cottage, sad in heart for her sister.

At one thirty in the morning of the 31st October, the storm broke with earnest. The full moon, at times covered by the darkest of clouds, competed with the fork lightening which ravaged the sky accompanied by heavy rolls of thunder. The fifty-foot waves crashed mercilessly against the rocks surrounding the small cove. Nothing was spared by the cruelty of the sea. Boats high up on the beach, assumed to be out of harm's way, were lifted up by the waves then dashed against the rocks and splintered into driftwood. This would be collected for kindling at the earliest opportunity to top up fires needed in the winter months. One person's loss was another man's salvation.

At nineteen minutes pass two exactly, a thunderbolt struck the roof of Agastine's cottage. In an act of defiance to the weather, Erasmus entered the world.

Chapter 2

The timing of Erasmus's birth was crucial. Fate had decreed that he would be born on a predicted date and time to coincide with the birth of a young woman in another era.

This was not his first life on this earth though; there had been others through many aeons of time. Erasmus, of course, was not aware but this lifetime would be the most significant of all. He had been predestined with special gifts and these would begin to materialise around the age of pubescence.

Erasmus was a beautiful child, born with masses of curly black hair. He had large, penetrating, blue eyes with long black eyelashes which formed a fringe to cover them. Wherever his parents took him he always commanded attention both from women and men. His smile lit up his face but, when chastised or reprimanded, a black scowl would appear and his blue eyes would turn almost black. Some folk, called it the evil eye when out of earshot of his family.

The only blemish Erasmus received at birth was a small mark at the base of his spine.

By his fifth birthday, although beloved by his parents, his sisters had grown wary of him and tended to stay out of his way whenever possible. If they upset him he would say nothing but just stare at them. His eyes seemed to penetrate the depths of their souls.

Family members and friends who could spare him some time took on his education mostly from his home.

During his free hours in the spring and summer months, Erasmus wandered along the beach by himself regardless of the weather, amusing himself by studying the flotsam washed up by the tide. He was completely independent and preferred his own company from this early age and he knew no harm could come to him provided he didn't venture too near the sea edge. The seas surrounding the Devon and Cornish coastline were notoriously dangerous at certain times of the year and one hundred foot waves were not unusual in the depths of winter.

As time went on, his confidence grew and he undertook to educate himself where possible with help from his family when it suited them. He seemed to be mature beyond his years and his parents' pride in him was self-evident, and he in turn returned their love.

At the age of seven however he suffered a major blow when his father was killed in an accident. He had been collecting salvage from a ship blown off course during bad weather. A rope had been securely tied at one end to a metal ring which was embedded in a rock on the shoreline and the other end had been tied round his waist. The pounding of the waves had loosened the rope around his waist and he was washed out to sea. His body had never been found.

Erasmus was inconsolable for many months and even his sisters took pity on him. Eventually he realised that he would have to take over the responsibility of his family and earn enough to keep the family together. He began to rise with the dawn and take to his bed at sunset, earning money where he could but taking time to pour over his beloved charts at every opportunity.

He could predict the weather with remarkable accuracy by the time he was nine by merely studying the skies. He even made his own simple charts, which impressed his elders.

Erasmus spent many hours alone but he never felt lonely and this would hold good for the rest of his life.

Chapter 3

During winter nights, when the family sat around a roaring fire, he would make new charts, which now included the stars' movements as well as those of the sun, moon and tides. Because of the accuracy of his work Erasmus had earned the respect of the fishing community. Fish was one of the mainstays of their diet and a good catch meant full stomachs.

During this time his sisters would fashion seashells into necklaces and other trinkets, partly for amusement but mostly to sell in the markets around the coast. When the sea was calm they were allowed to go in their own small boat to the next cove where a midweek market was held.

On the eve of his tenth birthday he was walking along the beach around the bay. His charts were under his arm, and he looked for a suitable rock to sit on whilst studying. A couple of local girls called Viorena and Clarissa, whom he knew to be sisters, came towards him.

They were about his age but he only knew them vaguely. Erasmus hated to be disturbed and most of all by any females. Having six sisters was bad enough and he considered them all to be beneath him. This set his black mood. By now he knew that when he was angry his eyes turned black and some folk were fearful of this. It was his secret weapon.

Recently, though, he had discovered something else that he was keeping to himself. If he concentrated hard he could read people's thoughts. It had frightened him at first and he wanted to tell his mother but something stopped him. He enjoyed the power it gave him even in his tender years. Many times he had used it to his advantage and now as the girls approached him they started to laugh and to taunt him.

"How be Erasmus? Still making out your silly charts?" Viorena asked.

"Can you make the moon come out during the day Erasmus?" Clarissa asked.

"You stupid children," he said in a very grown-up manner. "The moon is frequently out during the day but you can't always see it".

"My dad," went on Viorena going in for the kill," says the moon only comes out at night to light our paths."

"Enough!" screamed Erasmus, his eyes turning as black as coal. His face in a mask of hatred, he stared at both of them in turn. As he did so they both began to rise slowly from the ground and floated several steps backwards before landing back on their feet again. The two girls went white with shock. Terrified and shaking, they cowed away, turned and ran.

Erasmus, although surprised by what he had achieved, was secretly pleased and the laugh he gave turned into a heinous cackle. So it begins, he thought. Unsure why he had made the remark, but pleased with it, he turned back to his work and charts.

Chapter 4

In the intervening years, until his sixteenth birthday, he matured into a very good looking man. Many women chased after him but he was indifferent to them. His only female interest was his mother who had never remarried after the death of his father although she had many suitors.

Many times she remarked to Erasmus "He was my one love and so it shall be until we are joined again."

His sisters, who were all older than him, had married by now and left home. He was an uncle many times over and in his opinion he intended to stay single. Women were a curse and a nuisance and he didn't need them in his life.

By the time he reached his twenty-first birthday his opinion of women had not altered. He had already achieved the experience of being with a woman. He had used her and then cast her aside. He had also realised the potential of his good looks. Woman almost literally swooned at his feet and he had his pick of many when it suited him.

His mother, Agastine, was in the depths of despair. The beautiful boy that she had reared with such love and devotion seemed to be turning into a monster. He treated women with distain and she could not understand this at all. She decided to visit Tula the soothsayer and allow her to show her the future. Many times she had visited her in the hope of making contact with her beloved sister Drendell, but so far to no avail.

She made her way along the seashore wrapped in a long warm cloak. The hood, which was tied at the neck, protected her head from the bitter cold wind coming off of the sea. Never mind, she consoled herself; the warmth of fine spring days was just around the corner.

Tula lived in an isolated cave set back in the rocks which formed part of the cliff. She had deliberately chosen the cave because she preferred her own company and it was also protected from the ravages of the violent winter storms. All she needed she had around her.

Agastine had to negotiate a couple of large slippery rocks and then climb upwards to reach Tula, but she enjoyed her company and the climb was always worthwhile.

The entrance to the cave was very low. Agastine had to bend almost double to get in but thereafter it opened out to a large cavernous space where she was able to stand erect. Although there was a feel of damp about the cave, the large fire gave off warmth and took away the immediate chill. To one side were the remains of a meal that Tula had cooked over the fire and, on the other side, on an old white cloth that was now blackened with age and had seen better days, were her crystal ball and the animal teeth she cast to tell the future.

Agastine looked around but could not see Tula at all. Maybe she was at the back of the cave in her bed, thought Agastine.

"Ah, Agastine, I have been expecting you, my dear," said a voice from somewhere off to the left.

Agastine jumped.

"Tula, you surprised me," she said, still unable to see her and waiting for her eyes to adjust to the dark.

Instantly a woman wearing a long black dress with an old woollen shawl round her shoulders appeared in front of her. Her long straggly but surprisingly clean hair hung around her shoulders.

"Come and sit down here with me on this blanket, Agastine. We can warm ourselves by the fire."

Agastine did as she was told. She had the greatest respect for the talents of the woman and also considered her a true friend. Tula had befriended her when her sister had been killed.

"So, Erasmus is it then?"

Agastine was no longer shocked that the woman could see what was on her mind without asking.

"Yes, Tula, he has changed so much. What do you see for him?"

The old woman looked into the crystal ball which had been cloudy but had now cleared.

"The timing of his birth was crucial as it coincided with the birth of a beautiful young woman, but I will come back to that in a moment. Firstly we will talk of his powers which you are unaware of."

As Tula looked into the crystal ball, she could see an image of Erasmus. He had grown much taller since she had last seen him. His black curly hair was shining in the sunlight and came over his forehead just reaching his eyebrows. It hung at the nape of his neck where it flicked upwards but in a random manner. Yes, she thought, I can see why many maidens would want to run their hands through his hair. His body was now lean but very muscular, an attribute made obvious by the tight fit of his clothes.

"Well, Tula, what is it that can you see?" Agastine asked impatiently.

What Tula saw in the crystal ball disturbed her. She decided to confirm it by casting the teeth, an ancient form of rune stones. Confirmation was given to her in what they showed. How on earth do I tell his mother, she thought? She had always given to the querent whatever she saw in the ball but this was a bit different.

Firstly Tula decided she would tell her about the woman born at the same time as Erasmus, which would give her time for a decision.

"Well, Agastine," she began, "at the exact moment of Erasmus's birth, in another land and time, a baby girl was born. Her given name is Shasta and she is also predestined for many things. Their lives will run on a parallel course until, at a time chosen by fate, they will meet."

Over the next two hours Tula told her everything that she could see, leaving nothing out. Agastine listened intently. From past experience she knew that Tula would now be exhausted.

Rising, she reluctantly left the fire's warmth. She wrapped her cloak round her, said goodbye, and slowly walked back to her cottage. Her thoughts were in turmoil. Over and over she thought about what Tula had told her.

This Shasta was a very gentle woman and she and Erasmus would apparently meet very soon.

She felt mixed emotions about her son's future and by the time she had reached the cottage she felt exhausted. The wind was at its strongest and it left her thin body chilled to the bone.

Inside the cottage she removed her cloak and warmed herself by the fire. The cooking pot, suspended from a chain and hook deep within the chimneybreast, gave off a wonderful aroma of broth. She took down a mug and filled it to the brim. Whilst warming her hands on the mug, she slowly sipped the contents. Eventually it began to seep its warmth even through to the deep chill of her bones.

Sitting back in her chair and momentarily closing her eyes she relaxed her body ravaged by constant childbirth. She loved each of her children equally, but Erasmus had crept into her soul. She always knew he was destined for greater things from the moment he first moved inside her. Time will tell, she thought, as she drifted into a fitful sleep.

Chapter 5

"No one can touch me. I am omnipotent!" screamed Erasmus to the roaring waves as they splashed him with salt spray.

He was feeling especially good today. Facing the sea with hands held up high, he shouted it again for good measure. He loved days when the wind roared and whipped up the sea to a frenzy. Turning his back to the sea, he began climbing up on to the rocks and walked towards his special cave. It was situated at the bend of the cove and he had chosen it deliberately because no one ventured this far. Set back in the rocks it took some finding. On one occasion he had walked past it and, if he could miss it, so would others.

Taking a final quick look around him he ducked inside the cave. As with most of these caves it was set above water level and perfectly dry. Once through the entrance there was ample room to stand straight. Looking around he viewed everything with satisfaction. Near the entrance was a large pile of kindling wood gathered after a recent storm which he topped up as stocks got low. The remains of a previous fire faced towards the entrance. He had checked and double-checked that no one could approach from the back of the cave and surprise him. Beside the fire was a bedroll as occasionally he worked long into the night and slept there.

In neat piles, on oilcloths, were his beloved charts. Here he could work in peace without disturbance. His mother had challenged him many times about staying away but he just shrugged her off. On bright mornings at sunrise he often just sat at the cave entrance watching the sea ebb and flow. Occasionally he caught a fish for breakfast with a crude rod and line.

He let out a satisfied sigh. He was happy. No woman had invaded his inner sanctum and none ever would. If he felt like their company, he would go into the village and he was never short of offers.

Tonight he would work late and then rise with the dawn.

Feeling a chill about his body he relit the fire, topping it up gradually with the kindling wood. As the fire took hold and warmed him, he began to feel sleepy. He found himself unconsciously focusing on the flames. After a few moments they seemed to dance before his eyes, leaving him almost in a trance. He had experienced this before but not to this intensity, so he allowed his body and mind to go along with it. Suddenly the flames seemed to part slightly and within the smoke a vision appeared.

Erasmus was mesmerised. He could see a large opulent room which he realised was a bedroom. There were many coloured drapes hanging from the ceiling to floor. On a large four-poster bed, which was covered in a silk counterpane, was the most beautiful woman he had ever seen. Delicately dressed in sky blue, her tiny feet uncovered, she lay there sleeping. Her long blonde hair was dressed in a plait which lay over her shoulder, bound at the end in blue ribbon and resting on her bosom. Her long blonde eyelashes in sleep were curled but still covered her eyes. As he continued to watch the vision, his strength ebbed from him and he felt weak, a completely new experience for him. He could not take his eyes from the woman. For the first time he was experiencing love and knew he had to possess this woman whoever she was. He would find a way and wouldn't give up until he succeeded.

His ability to read minds didn't hold as much interest these days and it became boring to him. Recently, though, he had discovered, whilst sitting quietly in his cave and meditating, that he could transport his body through time. On one occasion he had decided to visit the village merely by thinking about it. His body was still in the cave but to all intents and purposes his being was in the village walking about holding conversations when it suited him. He cackled to himself at the thought. Whoever this beautiful woman was he intended to have her.

He sat back and watched the vision slowly fade as Shasta stretched her lithesome body and opened her eyes. For a moment she seemed startled and then the flames replaced all that he had witnessed.

Chapter 6

Shasta sat bolt upright in her bed. The dream had seemed almost real. The man was about her age and very good looking. His eyes had transfixed her, penetrating to the depths of her soul.

She wished he had been real, as her life seemed pretty mundane and she was bored. Men had come and gone in her life but none of them had excited her.

In the evenings she usually sat at home with her closest friends or, on warm evenings, in her beautiful garden. Flowers grew in abundance and the heady perfume was intoxicating during the hot summer evenings.

On many occasions, to amuse her friends, she would predict the future for them. However it bored her after a while and many times it tired her too. She had tried to close her mind to the gift but to no avail. She needed a new challenge and the man in her dream looked as if he could possibly fulfil it.

Rising from her bed, she breakfasted on fruit and sweet meats and decided to visit the market place. As she wandered, she became aware, as always, of admiring glances both from men and women. Some wished her good day while others passed her by with a friendly smile.

Seeing a woman sitting on the ground casting teeth, she grew curious and began to approach her. She was aware of soothsayers but had never actually met one. Unfamiliar with the practice of waiting until called, Shasta forced her way through, receiving some hostile looks. The soothsayer beckoned her forward, though, and said "Sit with me awhile, Shasta. I have much to tell you."

"How did you know my name"? Shasta asked aghast.

"I have been waiting for you for many years, my child, and finally you are here."

Shasta was full of questions.

"All in good time," said the woman who by now was casting the teeth again in front of her.

Shasta asked her what she should call her.

"My name is Liana," she said quietly.

Shasta moved a bit closer so that she wouldn't have to strain to hear her.

Slowly the other folk who had gathered to have readings moved away to return another day. They sensed that this woman would be there a long time.

Liana sat quietly for a few moments and then began to speak to Shasta.

"You were given many gifts at your birth, Shasta, but this man of your dreams holds your full interest at the moment." Shasta was startled, unable to speak. "He is called Erasmus and, like you, possesses many gifts. He was born at the exact moment of your birth but in another time. Your paths are predestined to cross when the time is right. He will love you to the point of obsession, and will travel through time to be by your side".

Liana stayed quiet for a few moments to enable Shasta to take this in. She decided against telling her too much too soon as she knew that Shasta would return to speak with her again.

Shasta rose to her feet in a trance but, recovering herself, thanked the old woman and walked further on to gather her thoughts. Her mind was in turmoil with so many unanswered questions.

Eventually she found herself at the back entrance to her house. Unlatching the gate, she wandered through the garden and sat on a bench beneath the arbour. The heady perfume of the white roses did nothing to deter her thoughts.

Restlessly she began to walk the garden back and forth, weighing a multitude of questions, the two foremost being who was this Erasmus, and how would he come through time to meet her?

On and on the questions invaded her mind until she finally accepted the fact that she was excited by the prospect of meeting him. The last thought in her mind as she closed her eyes that night was whoever Erasmus was, he was certainly good looking.

She fell into a troubled sleep, tossing back and forth amid visions of Erasmus travelling through space and time to be by her side.

These dreams occurred on a regular basis over the next few weeks and she knew in her heart that she would return to the market place and to Liana to find out more.

Chapter 7

Erasmus was pouring over his charts in his cave. Beside him the fire was getting low but he was warm enough and content. Outside the wind howled and the rain beat mercilessly against the rocks which formed the cave.

Occasionally he would stiffen like an alert animal, convinced that he could hear footsteps, but then he would relax again in the realisation that it was probably a combination of the wind and the rain.

Stretching his stiffened limbs, he stood and flexed his muscles. In his makeshift mirror he gazed at his profile, turning this way and that. He was proud of his toned body and knew that any woman would be happy to be bedded by him. Erasmus had become vainer as the years had gone by and realised that he also had the ability to attract men when the mood took him.

He threw more wood on the fire and sat down to watch contentedly as the smoke curled into the air. He knew that he would have another vision if he looked into the flames long enough.

Sure enough, as he watched, the smoke of the fire cleared to reveal a garden right there before him, with flowerbeds overflowing with beautiful plants whose heady perfume he readily imagined. Further along, beneath a rose arbour and seated on a bench, was the woman of his dreams. He viewed her in profile, her head slightly bent in contemplation, sitting composed with her hands lightly resting in her lap. Her long blonde hair was gently flowing about her shoulders and, as the gentle breeze caught it, wisps of hair moved across her face. She was dressed in an equally flowing red dress and her dainty feet peeped out from underneath the hem.

Again Erasmus sat spellbound as he watched. Mentally he wondered about her name. As the thought passed through his mind he instantly knew it to be Shasta. Yes, it fitted her perfectly, he thought; she seemed as pure as the white Shasta daisy grown in abundance. He was even more determined to possess her.

He instantly made up his mind to transport himself to her time.

Letting the vision go, he closed his eyes and prepared himself mentally. He could watch everything in his cave from afar and, if need be, return instantly. Time travel has its compensations he said aloud to his surroundings.

With that, he transported himself but nothing happened. He was still in his cave. Panic set in, as this had never happened to him before. He tried again but still to no avail.

A deep rage began inside him and standing up he marched to the entrance to the cave. "How could this have happened? I am omnipotent," he roared.

Stepping outside to clear his head, he looked about in disbelief. Down below him on the shore were men and women chattering and laughing. A dog was running in and out of the sea retrieving sticks thrown by a young boy of indeterminate age.

Erasmus shielded his eyes from the strong sun which reflected off the sea, and looked on in amazement and horror. Where had all these people come from and didn't they know this was his part of the beach?

The men had rolled their trousers up to their knees and were cooling off in the sea. Women had tucked up their dresses and were playfully splashing the men, expecting the same in return.

Erasmus could not believe his eyes at first but then realised he had after all transported himself. This was evident by the clothes worn by the people around him and the difference in temperature. He was now in a time of warmth. Shasta he surmised was obviously living in the same place as him but at a time in the future.

What an extraordinary turn of events, he thought, and began to cackle heinously, which left his face with a contorted look. Very well then, he would explore the area and mentally compare the differences.

No one took any notice of the man walking by the rocks. His clothes generally weren't all that different from theirs and they were used to all kinds of hermits and holy men that lived in the caves, so he fitted in perfectly. Besides they were caught up in their own fun and amusement. Why should a stranger to these parts bother them?

Chapter 8

During the warm balmy days of summer, Shasta had taken to walking in and around the rocks surrounding the caves above the shoreline. Sometimes she discarded her shoes and paddled her feet in the sea, or sat by the small rock pools watching crabs and tiny fish scurrying about to reach cover away from prying eyes.

Today was beautiful, and walking barefoot in the sand she sought out her favourite rock which was situated above a cave.

She had become aware of the cave entrance when she had walked along the shoreline some time ago. On that occasion something had compelled her to look up and she had noticed something glinting in the sun by the entrance. Probably a piece of glass, she had thought, and put it out of her mind. Now, whilst sitting on the rock, she noticed the same piece of glass below her.

Curiosity got the better of her and she gradually eased herself over the rock to investigate. Picking it up, she realised it was a piece of clear quartz made smooth in all probability by the elements of time. It sat comfortably in her hand and she decided to keep it.

Returning to her rock she examined it more closely and held it up to the sun. She could see small facets which sparkled in the sunlight and pleased her. She placed it in her lap and then, resting back on her hands, she inclined her face to the sun to enjoy its warmth. Her mind wandered and her thoughts turned to Erasmus and when they would meet. Would it be soon, she wondered. Maybe it was time to go back and talk more with Liana.

The sun hid behind a puffball of cloud, casting a shadow across her face. Opening her eyes she decided to carry on her walk and take the long way back. She picked up the stone from her lap and held it in her hand. As she made her way home she began gently stroking the stone. It was quite unusual and fascinated her.

On reaching her home, Shasta went to the kitchen and placed the stone on the windowsill where it could catch the last rays of the day's sun and she could enjoy watching the prisms sparkle as its energy was recharged.

Her supplies of herbs were getting low, she noticed, as she prepared herself some broth. She would restock them when she visited the market tomorrow. It would also give her the opportunity to revisit Liana if she was there.

As she gazed into the remains of the broth, she became aware of a mist swirling around the inside of the bowl. Spellbound she watched as it cleared. A vision appeared of a man with his back to her looking out to sea.

"ERASMUS!"

This came out involuntarily from surprise as her heart began to beat faster. Then, as the scene shifted, she realised that he was standing just below her rock in front of the cave. At the same time she felt great foreboding and danger and instinctively knew that at some moment in time she would have to save him. From what, she had no idea.

Shaking uncontrollably, she sat back in the chair as the scene before her dissipated and the vision cleared to reveal the dregs of broth.

Sleep did not come easily that night and, on waking the following morning, the bedclothes were a tangled mess around her.

Maybe Liana would have some answers.

With hope in her mind she made her way to the market and purchased the herbs she required. As she slowly walked around she took in the natural ambience generated by a busy market on a warm day. Feeling calmer now, she began to smile at people, her smile being returned by women and men alike. She was after all a very beautiful woman.

Shasta became aware of a gentle sound behind her. Turning, she could see nothing that would make the sound, but there it was again. She chanced to look down and saw a very tiny black kitten which was seated on the ground expecting some sort of attention. As she squatted down beside it, the kitten looked at her with its head on one side. It began to scratch itself behind its ear whilst balanced on three splayed legs. Laughing, Shasta scooped it up and brought it level to her face so she could see it properly.

"What a pretty little thing you are," she said as the kitten put out a paw to touch her face.

Making some enquiries, she discovered that a family who could not afford to keep the litter had left it abandoned. Her soft heart went out to the black ball of fluff and she decided to keep it. She placed it in her basket on top of her soft shawl and the kitten snuggled down and went to sleep with a small sigh of contentment.

Buying some food and other necessities for her new charge she strode out with the purpose of finding Liana.

Coming across a small crowd, she saw Liana through a gap sitting on the ground. Shasta stayed at the back, content to wait her turn. Absentmindedly she began to stroke the cat whilst at the same time thinking of Erasmus.

"Well hopefully Liana can help out there," she said to none in particular. In the meantime she began to think of names for the kitten. Not knowing if it was male or female proved an added problem. She had never housed a pet before. Eventually the crowd cleared and Liana, seeing Shasta, beckoned her forward.

"Ah Shasta, I see Merlin has found you, then," she said on seeing the kitten.

"I don't understand," said Shasta. " What do you mean?"

"You will understand in time, my dear, but heed this warning. Erasmus will face danger," Liana said mysteriously.

Shocked by this statement, Shasta told Liana about her visions in the cup of broth.

"So it begins. He is here then." She carried on talking before Shasta could question her again. "Many times you will come close as ships in the night, until finally …." Liana stopped there, closed her eyes and let out a sigh. "True love never runs smooth, my dear Shasta, but have patience, Erasmus is Omnipotent, always remember that." Opening her eyes she said "Now go and enjoy Merlin while you can". She closed her eyes again and mentally left her surroundings.

Shasta had seen the soothsayer on two occasions now and each time had come away more confused than ever.

A scroll nailed to a building used as a meeting place caught her eye. Moving closer, she stroked Merlin's head. Reading the scroll, she noted that a talk would be given on astronomy and astrology the following afternoon. One hour would be dedicated to each subject with time for questions afterward. Shasta made up her mind to go. She had spent endless hours fascinated by the stars and this would be an opportunity to find out more.

Chapter 9

Erasmus walked along the shoreline for once mingling with the people, more out of curiosity than anything, but it also gave him the opportunity to eavesdrop on conversations. Many times he stopped very close to people on the pretext of looking out to sea. Bits of gossip caught his ears but he wasn't really interested.

Coming further inland he overheard two men talking about the tides and stars. Instantly his interest was gained.

"If only we could get a replacement," said one man who sounded quite educated to Erasmus.

"We will never find someone at such short notice to talk about astronomy and astrology" said the second in despair.

Erasmus introduced himself and enquired after their problem. It seemed that their speaker had let them down and could not be replaced in time as the talk was the following day. Giving a brief rundown of himself and his achievements, Erasmus offered his services which were gratefully accepted. They had no choice but to take a chance on him.

Receiving directions and the time of the venue, Erasmus bade them adieu and agreed to meet them the following day.

He cut short his walk and returned to his cave and, with excitement, began to prepare the charts he would need. No rehearsal was needed as his confidence knew no bounds.

As night began to draw in, Erasmus sat at the entrance to his cave. He was comfortable with his surroundings now that the bustle of the day had calmed, but very aware that he was in his own future which had seemed rather strange at first but he was growing accustomed to the notion. After all, somewhere here was the woman of his dreams and he was resolved to find her. Maybe she would attend the talk he would be giving tomorrow.

At this prospect he began to feel quite weak and his heart beat more rapidly. Unsure of the true meaning of love, he only knew that he must possess her body and soul whatever it took. With that thought he retired to his bed and whatever the following day would unfold.

Chapter 10

Shasta arrived home and, after feeding Merlin, she sat in her favourite chair in the kitchen. She placed her basket on the stone floor by her feet and watched the kitten clean himself with his paw.

"What a sweet little thing you are," she said.

Merlin stopped cleaning himself and appeared to be listening. He then walked across the floor, jumped into her basket and curled up. Resting his head on his now outstretched front paw, he let out a deep sigh of contentment and drifted into sleep. After a while he began to snore, much to Shasta's amusement.

Before retiring to bed that evening Shasta sat by her open kitchen door. It was wonderful to smell the sea air, mixed with the night perfume of all that grew in the garden. She felt a deep contentment.

Aware of the kitten by her feet, she picked him up and allowed him to select an unused part of the garden. Returning to her seat, she placed Merlin on her lap. With gentle stroking he began to purr which Shasta found very satisfying. How very comforting cats are, she thought.

That night she slept soundly.

The kitten in its adopted basket lay on Shasta's shawl knowing that he had been successful. Having found Shasta, his mistress, he now only had to find the Evening Star. That would probably be more difficult but he had all the time in the universe.

The following morning, Shasta awoke to see the sunshine coming in through her windows. She had not pulled the curtains the night before but instead had lain watching the star-studded sky until she drifted off to sleep.

Looking now to the side of the bed, she found Merlin awake watching her and, for a moment, it unnerved her. Although he was only a kitten, his eyes seemed to penetrate.

Suddenly feeling a bit stupid, she swung out of bed and stood by the window. Today, she reassured herself, would be a good day but, moments later, a sense of foreboding came over her for no reason and she felt cold.

Shaking it off, she scolded herself. "Stop being silly," she said with a firm resolve and, scooping up the basket along with Merlin, went down to the kitchen. Today she would learn about astronomy and astrology, an anticipation which happily sent her about her tasks.

Merlin loved Shasta's basket, deriving comfort from the warmth of her shawl. Sometimes he would play chase with the toys Shasta had made him but then, tiring, he would revert back to the basket and sleep.

This was how it was as Shasta prepared to attend the lecture. She scooped up the basket and made her way to the hall. Feeling a sense of excitement, she began to smile to herself and joined the throng of people making their way into the building.

The fixed seating was arranged in semi circles at different levels which enabled all of the audience to view the lecture area. The hall was already packed but, climbing the steps to the back of the auditorium, she was able to find a spare seat next to a rather rotund man. Due to the closeness of the seating, she found herself squashed between him and a large but friendly looking lady wearing a voluminous straw hat with cherries pinned on one side. The hat was worn at a rakish angle and, as she moved her head, it seemed to swivel with her.

Oh well, thought Shasta, at least I got a seat.

To keep an eye on Merlin, she placed the basket on her lap which brought forth "Ahs" and "Ohs" from the people in close proximity.

A hush came over the crowd and the speaker came to the table. He had an air of authority about him as he stood with his hands clasped behind his back surveying the audience. Although Shasta's seat was near the back she had a clear view of him. Her mouth dropped open in surprise, and her hands flew to her mouth to eradicate any sounds.

Before her was Erasmus. She only had to go back down the flight of stairs, walk forward and she could touch him. As this thought passed through her mind, Erasmus began to speak. His voice carried around the auditorium and he spoke with confidence and clarity. The hour seemed to rush by and then he took questions which he answered with complete authority. The audience was in no doubt; here was a man of great learning.

During this time Shasta was again able to study him. Once or twice, when the question came from her direction, he seemed to look straight at her, which caused her to blush. Then, after a five-minute break for a drink, he began again, this time discussing astrology and answering questions as his lecture progressed. When necessary, he pointed to relevant features on his charts which he had pinned to a board. The time went very quickly.

To cheers and rapturous applause, which Erasmus accepted as a matter of course, he walked off and out of sight. He didn't want to hang around. The intensity of the lecture had left him drained and tired.

As the hall began to empty, Shasta went down to the now empty table. Only the teacup remained on the table, and she tentatively picked it up. Erasmus had drained the cup dry and only the dregs were left in the bottom.

Automatically reading the dregs, she gasped with despair. The future did not look good for Erasmus and she saw danger from a source known to her.

Puzzled, she tried to read more but nothing was forthcoming. With concern, she replaced the cup back on the table and left.

Outside, the sun beat down with intensity and she realised how thirsty she was. Passing a vendor carrying fruit, she selected a large orange, peeled it and savoured the juice which on occasions dribbled down her chin, leaving a sticky residue.

As Merlin seemed quite content, she began to walk towards the beach to soothe her feet in the water. As she got close to a young skinny child begging near a doorway, Merlin sat bolt upright in the basket and began to meow pitifully. Then he tried to jump out.

Shasta put the basket down on the ground to settle him but he jumped out and sped towards the child and sat down beside him licking his foot. The child, who at first appeared to be withdrawn, began to laugh. Throwing a few coins to the child, she called Merlin to her but he wouldn't move. Instead he moved even closer to the child.

As Shasta tried to pick him up, he scratched her and she dropped him in surprise. What was wrong with him and why wouldn't he leave this child, she wondered.

Well, she couldn't stay here all day. Her gentle nature took over and she decided to take the child home, give him a good meal, then he could do whatever he willed.

The child indicated that he didn't understand Shasta's meaning. As her offer became clear to him, he reached for a stave lying on the ground.

Merlin, sensing that he was getting up, moved slightly out of his way. It took several moments for the child to raise himself and, as he began to walk, Shasta realised that he was crippled also.

Satisfied that the child was coming with them, Merlin jumped back into the basket in preparation. Shasta's pity went out to the boy. His affliction was bad enough but he had to survive by begging for alms. Well at least he would have a good meal tonight and maybe even a bed, provided he cleaned himself up first.

Whilst Shasta paddled her feet in the sea, the boy sat on the sand and played with Merlin who took great delight in rolling in the sand. The boy's happy laughter was a pleasure to hear and it caused Shasta to turn and watch them.

Something caught her attention as she glanced up towards the rocks. She imagined she saw Erasmus watching her but then decided it was her mind playing tricks.

When she came back and sat down, she decided to find out a bit more about the child and asked to know his name. Picking up a stone lying nearby he wrote in the sand the word HESPERUS and then, in brackets, (Hesper).

She was amazed that the child could write. He was probably no more than ten years old. He was usually called Hesper for short. By the time they left the beach, Shasta had not only ascertained his name but that he had always been able to read and write. He claimed that his parents had died in a fire, although his father's body had never been found. They were apparently very wealthy and owned a large house that had stood on an isolated rocky crag. Due to the isolation, no one was near enough to help put out the fire. He had looked after himself on the street for three years now and mostly he fed off of scraps thrown by well meaning individuals.

Shasta was confused by the boy's story. The house in question had been derelict for years, indeed for all of her lifetime. Nevertheless, whatever the truth, she was determined that tonight he would eat fit for a king and they slowly made their way back to her house.

Hesper had never really walked that far and was exhausted by the time they got to the house. He flopped in the kitchen chair nearest to him and promptly picked up Merlin who sat on his lap. Turning twice on Hesperus's lap, he settled down with a deep audible sigh.

Obviously they are both worn out, thought Shasta, and began to prepare a meal. Hesper closed his eyes from time to time and Shasta sensed she heard him mumbling to himself.

While the meal was cooking she sat in her garden and contemplated how she felt about the day. She had seen Erasmus and the dregs in the teacup showing danger from a source close to her. She began to wonder again who that could possibly be. No one in her circle of friends surely, and she wasn't aware of anything when she had done their readings.

Hesper, of course, and the way Merlin had reacted, that was certainly strange and she still bore the scratches he had given her.

Going back to the kitchen to attend to the food, she put it out of her mind for the time-being.

Waking Hesper who had fallen asleep, she suggested he might like to clean up as dinner was almost ready. With great reluctance, Merlin settled back in his basket. As Hesper went to clean up, Shasta registered that he did so with a quicker movement now that he was rested.

During dinner, Shasta and Hesper discussed many things and then, fed up with his constant pitiful cries, she put Merlin's basket at the end of the table near Hesper. They seemed to be becoming inseparable she thought to herself.

Out of curiosity Shasta asked Hesper if he knew why he had been called Hesperus.

"It means Evening Star. My mother was in our garden stargazing when I decided to enter the world. I entered too quickly and was born under the stars. Hesperus the Evening Star was shining brightest at the time so I was called Hesperus".

"What a lovely story," she said as she began to clear the dishes.

"May I take Merlin outside for a while, Shasta?" he asked, changing the subject.

"Certainly, but keep an eye on him as he likes to wander occasionally."

With his stave propped under his arm, and Merlin tucked under the other, he made his way outside.

Shasta made him a makeshift bed in the kitchen. The nights were very warm and he would be comfortable.

Listening to the happy laughter of the boy, she felt very sad in her heart for him. When they returned, Merlin settled himself on the bottom of Hesper's bed with no intention of moving. The boy with some difficulty slid in around him so as not to disturb him.

Saying goodnight to Merlin and then Shasta, he thanked her for her generous hospitality and settled himself for the night.

Obviously he had started to receive a good education, she thought, as she left him to his slumbers and went to her room.

Many thoughts went through Shasta's mind concerning the boy and she would make a decision in the morning.

In the kitchen the boy had only been feigning sleep and to the kitten he whispered "At last we have found one another. We are each other's strength and I vow we will never be separated again."

Merlin, on hearing this, crept up to Hesper's pillow and settled beside him with a small sigh of contentment.

Chapter 11

Erasmus walked back to his cave elated with his work and the response he received from the audience. Being so focused he had only been aware of a sea of faces in front of him. Some of the questions had intrigued him while others he considered were very naïve. What could he expect, though? These people were inferior to him.

He had been asked to give further talks in the future and he said he would consider it. He also knew that if he agreed he would never be left alone.

He had come to be with Shasta and that was his first priority. When he was lecturing in the hall he felt sure she was near but his mind was preoccupied with his subject.

As all these thoughts passed through his mind, he stood up and walked to the entrance of the cave. Then, bored with watching the water ebb and flow, he looked to the surrounding area. Generally it was quiet in the early evening with only the occasional person collecting driftwood thrown up by the tide.

He scanned the horizon slowly. In the distance he could make out an isolated house which seemed to be balanced on the hillside. From this distance it seemed to look neglected and derelict. He made up his mind to have his meal and to take a walk up to view it more closely. The sun usually set over that way so it would be very pleasant. Maybe it would be useful he thought, but not really sure what for.

As he strode out towards the house, he thought he could see someone in the distance. They seemed to be walking the same way. He cursed under his breath but still carried on walking.

Approaching the house, he realised that it was mostly a ruin. The roof and stone outer walls had stood the test of time and the inner layout gave a rough impression of the various rooms in the house which had been weathered by nature. Erasmus got the impression that it might prove to be of some use to him in the future as it seemed quite dry inside. Satisfied, he walked back outside and toured the perimeter once more. As he turned the corner, he bumped straight into Shasta who, preoccupied, had not seen him.

Recognising him, her hands flew to her mouth in embarrassment. Erasmus, more in control but nevertheless surprised at seeing Shasta so unexpectedly, recovered more quickly.

"Good evening, Mistress. Please excuse my tardy manners and accept my apologies for causing you distress."

With a gentle bob in acknowledgement, Shasta also apologised.

"My name is Erasmus. May I enquire after yours?" he asked with amusement.

"If you please, I am called Shasta, Sir," she said shyly.

Neither Shasta nor Erasmus gave any hint that they had knowledge of one another. Instead they remarked about each other's interest in the house and speculated as to what had happened to it.

Shasta explained that she had recently learned that there had been a fire at the house which was why it was now in ruins. She had come out of pure curiosity and had not expected finally to meet Erasmus at the same spot.

"But not a recent fire."

"No," Shasta replied. "It must have happened many years ago, before I was even born."

They mutually agreed to walk back together as they were going the same way.

As they walked, she admitted that she had been at his lecture that afternoon and declared her interest in the subject. Erasmus was both flattered and pleased and asked if they could meet later that evening. If she were agreeable he would explain the different clusters of stars to her. Shasta readily agreed and it was decided they would meet later when the sun had set.

Having reached her house, Erasmus remarked on its lavishness and the beauty of its garden and, with a cheery wave, left Shasta as she went into the garden to find Hesper and Merlin. Seeing them by the garden arbour, she stood for a while watching their antics. Hesper was balancing on one crutch and Merlin was attacking it then backing off and darting forward again. Hesper's laughter could be heard around the garden.

With a deep sigh she felt contentment in her decision to have the boy stay with her. He and Merlin had become inseparable now. It was as if they were one and Merlin had grown beyond recognition.

Shasta had gone to the ruin of the house Hesper claimed to have been his to satisfy her curiosity and to confirm in her mind that she had made the right decision. She had not entertained meeting Erasmus though. Excitement and slight fear were experienced at the same time. Realising she would have to prepare a meal and ensure her two charges were settled before she met Erasmus, she called out to them. Hesper came hobbling over to meet her, with Merlin walking sedately beside him on his best behaviour, unaware that Shasta had witnessed their previous game.

Over their meal she told Hesper of her meeting with Erasmus and for a split second a look of annoyance came over his face. She passed it off and they finished the rest of their meal in silence. Even Merlin had remained in the basket looking at her piercingly in that way that only a feline can.

As the evening was exceptionally warm, she wore her favourite silk midnight blue dress edged with silver. On her feet, peeping out from under the hem, was a pair of walking shoes which she used for the beach. Her hair was in two plaits

63

coiled over one another and pinned at the nape of her neck for coolness.

Leaving Hesper and Merlin together, Shasta made her way down the nearby path, which led to the beach. The tide was out in the cove, which pleased her as she loved to walk on the sand. Often she would take large strides and then stop, turn and check her footprints, which she did now. Coming up to a small rock pool she looked at the crabs and silver fish unaware that Erasmus was watching her.

Erasmus had been watching Shasta since she left her house. He hadn't realised how close she had been to him. The house could be seen from the outside of his cave and yet he had not realised it was hers.

He found this new experience very unnerving. He was used to being in complete control and nothing like this had happened to him before. From the moment he had first seen her in his vision, he'd felt weak to the core. Now, seeing her in the flesh, her dress shimmering in the moonlight and clinging to her like a second skin, left him feeling what......? He couldn't define it but he knew he felt vulnerable and he wasn't used to it. He was accustomed to having a complete upper hand with women.

As Shasta came closer, she saw him and he raised his hand in acknowledgement while she quickened her pace eager to shorten the distance between them.

Instantly feeling at ease in his company, she said "Good evening, Erasmus. Isn't this a beautiful evening?"

As Erasmus looked deep into her eyes, he thought they shone brighter than the moonlight and for a moment his heart quickened. Gathering himself together he agreed with her.

By mutual consent he took her arm and placed it in the crook of his. As they slowly walked the length of the beach, discussing the flora and fauna scattered about, Shasta noticed a piece of seaweed. She threw it at Erasmus and it landed on his shoulder. Sensing the fun element, he threw it back but his aim was off and it completely missed. For a split second he was angry with himself but then his anger was gone. Shasta was ready for the next attack and so it went on until they both ended up in the warm sea at waist level.

As Shasta's dress became wet around her legs it restricted her movements. This enabled Erasmus to move in to his advantage. Accepting the inevitable, Shasta turned to face Erasmus aware that he was getting closer.

The waves seemed to respect his efforts to get to her and, as he reached her, he just stood and looked at her as the water swirled about them. Taking hold of her plaited hair he arranged it to hang free around her shoulders. All the while he and Shasta maintained eye contact.

Putting his hand to her face, he encouraged her gently to come to him. As their bodies touched, he gently kissed her and, as passion took them both, they let the sea enfold their bodies.

As they waded out of the sea, their bodies still in close contact, Erasmus finally allowed a woman to invade his privacy by inviting Shasta to the warmth of his cave. The evening was still warm but the weight of her now soaking wet dress made it an easy decision for her and she acquiesced.

Slowly they climbed up to his cave and, once inside, he relit the fire while she removed her clothes. Erasmus produced a blanket to preserve her modesty then, with unexpected shyness on his part, he removed his own and wrapped another blanket around himself.

The warmth of the fire made them both drowsy and Shasta slowly settled against Erasmus. In time they lay down on the floor of the cave until sleep overcame them. Shasta now lay in the arms of Erasmus and, with a deep sigh, he allowed himself to succumb to slumber and there they stayed until morning.

Shasta at first couldn't work out why she couldn't move. She seemed to be pinned to the bed. Then she realised with horror that she was still in the cave and it was Erasmus keeping her body pinned, not to her bed, but to the floor.

As she moved, he awoke and was now looking straight into her eyes. As realisation dawned, he began to smile. He kissed her eyes and rolled on to his back, taking her with him. Contentedly he lay there watching her above him. Slowly kissing her mouth, he returned her back to her previous position. Recognising his intent, she tried to move, but he was too quick for her and once again she succumbed to him.

Finally he released her and, with healthy appetites, they breakfasted on fish from the sea which Erasmus cooked over the fire, and bread which they tore at ravenously.

As the hour was early and the sun only just beginning to rise, they sat at the mouth of the cave in companionable silence and watched the sea.

Erasmus, for the first time in his life, was deeply in love and along with his love came trust. He began to tell Shasta of his life from as far back as he could remember. When he had brought her up to date he felt an inner peace come over him. He knew that he would do anything for this woman and intended to get betrothed to her if she would have him. He was content to live in her lifetime and if he ever felt the need to go back to his own time, then the opportunity was there to do so.

Shasta enlightened him about her life and also explained how she had befriended Hesper and the cat.

Erasmus helped her to her feet and asked if he could walk back with her as far as her garden. She readily agreed to this.

As they approached the back gate, she decided to invite Erasmus inside for a drink and, as he didn't want to leave her just yet, he followed her in.

Hesper was still asleep on the floor in the kitchen. His crippled leg stuck out at an angle. Merlin was snuggled up on the pillow beside him. Shasta smiled with love at them, her new found family.

Erasmus, although unprepared to admit it, also felt an unusual feeling of tenderness, especially for the boy.

As Shasta turned to pour out a drink for them, Hesper awoke and, seeing Erasmus watching him, at first cowered away in fear. Recovering himself, he instantly replaced the fear with distain, which surprised Erasmus. He had crouched down to reassure the boy but, at this moment, Merlin awoke and began to hiss and spit at him and then flew at him, claws extended, and scratched his face.

Erasmus cried out in surprise more than pain. Shasta, who had witnessed most of the event, called out in disbelief. Scooping up Merlin she put him outside the door and began to attend to Erasmus's face. Hesper glanced at Erasmus and, with a satisfied look, went outside to join Merlin.

Neither Shasta nor Erasmus could understand the reactions of either of them. He had done nothing to provoke them. Indeed, he had tried to reassure Hesper that all was well. Merlin had seemed to react in defence of the boy. Fortunately the scratches were not deep and were easily cleaned.

Shasta decided to leave them outside whilst she and Erasmus drank thirstily. They could wait for their breakfast until later. At the same time she intended to see if she could get to the bottom of what had caused the reaction by Merlin. Hesper and he were inseparable these days. Maybe he had an answer for her.

Erasmus left Shasta, mutually agreeing to meet back on the beach in a couple of days. He noticed that the boy and cat were on the far side of the garden, so he took his leave and made his way back to the beach and his cave.

Shasta, having now prepared breakfast, called Hesper and Merlin back to the kitchen. Hesper appeared to be rather sullen and Merlin seemed reluctant to come in. So Shasta scooped him up and put him in front of his food. Sniffing it suspiciously, he began to eat.

"Why were you afraid of Erasmus, Hesper?" she asked as he began to eat.

"I wasn't afraid of him," he said defiantly.

"Is there anything wrong?" she asked, determined to get to the truth.

"No!" he said with emphasis.

"Hesper, you have to understand that Erasmus is my friend and he will be coming to visit us frequently," she said trying a softer approach.

Well, thought Hesper, maybe that would be to my advantage, so I will play along.

Aloud to Shasta he said "I'm sorry for my behaviour. I will apologise to Erasmus when I see him, but I have come to like living with you and I thought maybe you would want me to leave if he was here."

Instantly her face softened and he knew he had achieved his goal.

"Oh Hesper, I would never ask you to go. You're now part of this family along with Merlin. You may stay as long as you wish."

With an exaggerated sigh he thanked her. Merlin reacted accordingly and began to purr loudly.

Well thank goodness that is sorted out she thought, and began to clear the dishes.

Chapter 12

As Erasmus walked down towards the beach he whistled, happily pleased with life.

He was still surprised at the way the cat had struck but he could ignore that because he was in love. Yes! He could finally admit it to himself. The light-hearted feeling took some getting used to though.

His happy demeanour must have been infectious because he realised he was smiling at passersby and actually said good morning to them and, for the first time, meant it.

As he walked along the sand he took off his shoes and paddled his feet in the water. Looking out to sea he shouted at the waves,

"I'm in love and I don't care who hears me."

A passing stranger raised his cap and expressed his congratulations.

Oh boy did he feel good. All these years this is what had been missing from his life. Always he had used women to suit his needs but this was so different.

Shasta was beautiful in nature and body and he was determined to permanently make her his.

Going back to his cave he found that he was hungry again and ate his last piece of bread. Deciding he would have to go to the market, he set out once more bidding everyone good day and receiving pleasant salutations back.

Why haven't I done this before, he thought. I have always felt so superior to others and they aren't that bad really. In fact they seem quiet nice.

Having collected his provisions he decided to have a proper look around. He bought some ribbons for Shasta's hair and a new shirt for Hesper. To pacify Merlin, he bought him a wooden mouse on a string attached to a stick.

Moving on, he was aware of people sitting patiently on the ground in front of an old woman. Walking towards them he decided to sit and listen. The woman, he deduced, was called Liana and she was a foreseer. He wondered why he hadn't noticed her before.

He decided to sit and watch for a while as he had made no plans for today.

One by one as they took their turn, she cast the teeth on the ground in front of her and spoke of their future to them.

Erasmus was fascinated as to how she could read anything from old teeth and stones. He recalled his mother going to see a foreseer when he was much younger, and she had tried to explain to him how people were able to see the future. At the time he accepted it as he did his own gifts, and never really thought any more about it. He had felt his own gifts to be far superior, although they were completely different to this. Now he thought about it, he had been so happy today, just accepting people for who they were. He had not even tried to read their minds and, somehow, had started to treat them as his equals. He wasn't sure how he felt about this and, as he began to consider it, he realised it was finally his turn to meet the woman.

Stepping forward in front of Liana he sat down again.

Liana had been aware of Erasmus sitting waiting and, if truth be told, she had to admit surprise. He was certainly a handsome man beyond anything she had imagined. She could well understand why so many women had been constantly turning their heads to take a second look and receive a smile.

Now, in turn, she found herself smiling into his eyes which gave her the impression of deep pools of liquid.

"Well, Erasmus, so you come at last!"

Covering his surprise well he said "How do you know my name?"

"I know everything, Erasmus. I also know that you have finally met Shasta and she is everything that you have ever dreamed of."

This time he couldn't cover his surprise as she was quick to notice. She decided not to comment and, instead, carried on as if nothing had happened.

"The exact moment of your birth was predestined to be 31st October at nineteen minutes past two in the morning. Shasta was also born at the same time and on the same date, but many years in the future. Fate decreed that you would travel to the future to find her and fall in love."

"But why has this happened, Liana? Yes, it's true, I love Shasta. In fact, I have never been happier. I have discovered that I actually enjoy talking to people and I can now look on them as my equals instead of feeling superior to them."

"Ah, such are the vagaries of fate, Erasmus. Humility and tolerance are the greatest of gifts." Suddenly Liana grabbed his arm. "Beware; in loving Shasta, you may suffer the consequences! Now go."

With that, she dropped her head and appeared to go to sleep. Erasmus tried to question her further but he realised that she seemed to be in a kind of trance.

Reluctantly he got up and, picking up his provisions, he made his way back.

Yes, he thought, I have started to consider the feelings of others and I admit it does make me feel good. What did she mean though when she said I would suffer the consequences? He had tried to read Liana's mind, but unsuccessfully. "How very strange," he said out loud to no one in particular, but he didn't think too much of it. He would be seeing Shasta soon and that made up for everything. He resolved to make her a surprise visit earlier than planned and deliver his gifts.

The next day he arose at dawn, cooked breakfast and sat outside his cave watching the spectacular sunrise. By midday it was extremely hot and the beach filled with families making the most of the low tide and the opportunity to cool off. The happy shrieking voices he heard reminded him of the evening spent with Shasta, and her happy squeals of laughter. He mentally ran over his feelings once more marvelling at the way he felt. He couldn't wait to see her again.

When it cooled off later, he would go to see her. He hoped she and her little family liked his gifts. Funny he thought how he looked on them as a family. Perhaps soon they would become his family.

Lying back against a rock with his hands folded behind his head he squinted slightly due to the sun and surveyed with delight the many families around him. With a satisfied sigh he drifted into sleep.

He was awoken from his slumbers by two men deep in conversation close by.

"Perhaps we should wait until he awakes," said one.

"Well, we need to speak to him soon if we are going to obtain his services," said another.

Opening his eyes slightly he said "Can I be of service gentlemen?"

"Indeed, Sir. We understand that you are learned in the charts of the stars and heavens. You are the man that lectured in the hall a while back."

"Yes, that is correct. How can I help you?"

"Well if it isn't too much trouble, Sir, we are holding informal talks in the market place and we wondered if you would help us out by attending. If there are questions that we can't answer, maybe you can help."

Erasmus, obtaining more details of the event, agreed to go. His interest was heightened because it was to be held close to where Liana held her readings. There would be plenty of time to sort out his charts if he needed them at a later time. Anyway most of his information was in his head.

Going back into the cave he picked up his gifts and made his way to Shasta's house.

As he approached the garden he heard her laughing with Hesper. Peering at them from under the cover of some bushes, he watched them playing with a ball. Merlin was also joining in. Suddenly Merlin arched his back and his hair stood on end. He was looking off to the end of the garden. Shasta looked amazed. Whatever was wrong with him? Hesper also looked startled.

As he stroked his fur, he asked "Merlin, what is it? What's wrong?"

Somehow he expected an answer from him.

Looking in the same direction as the cat, he realised it was Erasmus. He wasn't as well hidden as he thought.

"It's Erasmus," was all he said. Scooping up Merlin he made his way inside.

Shasta's reaction was completely the opposite. She ran to the end of the garden and let him in. Demurely gave him a kiss which was returned by Erasmus with passion, momentarily taking her breath away.

"Hello, Erasmus. I wasn't expecting you today."

"I hope you don't mind. I have some gifts for you," he said.

"Oh how lovely. Come inside and we can look at them."

They walked arm in arm inside, to find Hesper sitting in the chair with a sullen look on his face and Merlin on his lap.

"Oh what's this?" she asked surveying the scene. "Hesper, I believe you wanted to say something to Erasmus when you next saw him?"

For a moment Hesper looked taken back. The last thing on his mind was to apologise, but he had agreed and he had to keep up the pretence of friendship, at least for the time-being. His chance would come soon enough.

"Erasmus, please forgive me for being so rude on your last visit. I thought Shasta would ask me to leave if she became friendly with you, and I was jealous."

There, it was said, he thought to himself. Not a word of the apology was meant but Erasmus and Shasta didn't know that.

"Think no more about it, Hesper. I have a gift for you here. See if you like it."

Handing the shirt to him, Erasmus suddenly realised he hadn't thought about size and hoped that it fitted. As luck would have it, when Shasta helped him hold it up against his small frame it did.

As he gave the ribbons to Shasta, he first held them to her hair to see the effect and decided they looked beautiful.

"I haven't forgotten you, Merlin" he said as he produced the mouse on the stick.

Merlin, who was now on the floor, couldn't resist the challenge and jumped several feet in the air trying to catch it, but Erasmus was too quick and lifted it higher out of his way, to much accompanying laughter, even from Hesper.

Erasmus gave him the toy and suggested they went outside to play with it. Judging by Hesper's noisy expressions of amusement, it was an instant success.

Erasmus and Shasta stood looking at one another, savouring the moment. Eventually Erasmus broke the silence.

"I can't believe how happy you make me feel, Shasta. I love you so dearly. Will you accept my betrothal?"

Shasta was at first overwhelmed by his sudden proposal, but soon agreed with alacrity. Sealing the betrothal with a kiss, they went out to tell Hesper, unsure of his reaction.

They were left with no doubt that Hesper didn't approve. He turned his back on them and hobbled on his crutch to the bottom of the garden. He went out through the gate and started to make his way to the beach.

Shasta and Erasmus left it a while and then followed at a discreet distance. They mutually agreed to reassure the boy that he would have a permanent home with them.

Merlin padded back into the kitchen. He got in his basket, curled up and, with deep satisfaction, went to sleep.

Erasmus and Shasta finally caught up with Hesper down on the beach. By now it was dusk and the Evening Star had appeared alongside the moon. Hesper was sitting on a rock on the beach gazing at it intently. Of course, thought Erasmus, making the connection, he was called after the Evening Star, Hesperus. He related his thoughts to Shasta and she confirmed them.

He doesn't realise it, thought Erasmus, but we have a lot in common.

As they approached the boy he tried to make off. Erasmus stopped him.

"What is wrong, Hesper? Can't we be friends?"

Hesper thought quickly and decided he would have to dissemble if he were to achieve his goal.

"I'm sorry, Erasmus. I've been so lonely all my life and Shasta has made me feel part of her family. I thought that maybe you wouldn't want me to stay now that you're friends."

Hopefully Erasmus will accept that explanation he thought to himself.

"Hesper, it's true that Shasta and I are friends. Actually I have asked her if she will become betrothed to me and she has agreed. But we would like you to stay living with us if that's acceptable to you?"

Well this couldn't have worked out better, he thought to himself.

Out loud he said "Oh, Erasmus, I don't know what to say. I'm so grateful to you both. Thank you." And with a few heartfelt sobs thrown in for good measure, he hid his face in Shasta's dress while she patted his head with genuine affection.

"You and I have a lot in common, Hesperus," said Erasmus using his full name and trying to ease the situation. I am very interested in the heavens and the stars and you are called after the Evening Star. How did you come by that name?"

Swayed for a moment by the discovery of mutual ground, Hesper explained what had happened with his birth.

Erasmus laughed with genuine amusement at this and for a long while the three of them sat in companionable silence watching the stars and picking out the most significant ones. Erasmus was genuinely surprised at the knowledge shown by Hesper.

Eventually they walked back to Shasta's house and, for the first time for as long as he could remember, Erasmus didn't sleep in his cave.

Although he didn't realise it, Erasmus, through love, was beginning to weaken and lose some of his strength.

Hesper, settling down beside Merlin, agreed that this was working out better than they expected.

Chapter 13

The following days were spent in idyllic harmony. Hesper now seemed to accept the regular visits of Erasmus and, when Shasta wasn't at home, he fended for himself and Merlin quite happily.

Erasmus went to the talks in the market and took Hesper along with him. When questions were asked of him, Erasmus often referred the questioner to Hesper who always seemed to have the correct answer. At one point Hesper seemed almost as much in demand as Erasmus.

Erasmus was however in love and that was the most important thing on his mind, day or night. He had not even considered for some time now that he was living in a different time to his own. His only thought was his love for Shasta.

She at first neglected her friends in favour of Erasmus but then the realisation hit her one day when she was sitting in her garden with no one around to talk to that they were equally important and she began to invite them back again. Many evenings she sat in her garden doing readings for them as before and relating stories of how her life had changed and the difference Erasmus and Hesperus had made. Frequently they played with Hesper, encouraging him to take part but also being mindful of his handicap. In his own way, Merlin joined in causing frequent squeals of laughter at his antics.

Shasta accepted a lot of teasing from her friends concerning her love at first sight and the fact that they were jealous of her. But they all agreed on the fact that they certainly complimented one another.

Erasmus, for his part, took to Hesper completely and tried to include him in everything he did. Hesper was a quick learner and admitted to Erasmus that he often had studied the stars himself as a child.

Hesper went along with everything Erasmus suggested. In fact he quite enjoyed being involved with the informal lectures that now seemed to be more frequent. He often found he was able to answer questions off the top of his head while Erasmus was busy consulting his charts.

Hesper was biding his time, knowing that his time would come soon enough.

Chapter 14

Hesper took to visiting the ruins of his old house on the craggy rock more regularly now. Since making his new home with Shasta, he felt more secure. Sometimes Merlin would tag along, content to sit beside him with his head resting between his front paws. Now that he was bigger he had become more adventurous, but he knew his limitations and boundaries.

Hesper sat on the ground within the walls looking for past comforts and trying to remember the day-to-day routine of his parents. It was as if it had only happened three years ago but it seemed an eternity.

With the warmth of the sun on his face he closed his eyes and looked back as far as he could remember.

He remembered the endless games his mother played with him. That was foremost in his mind and he loved her dearly. His father was away from the house on a regular basis and he recognised even at his tender age that his mother got lonely and sad at times. Occasionally she was visited by a man who never seemed to be empty handed. There were always presents for his mother and these usually included something unusual for him. On many occasions he felt there was something unsettling about this man but he accepted him anyway because he made his mother happy. She explained that they had been friends for many years and she had known him long before she met his father and he must always be as respectful to him as he was to his father.

Hesper thought it strange though that he only seemed to visit when his father was away.

When his father was at home, his mother was never without a smile. She would hug him and his father constantly. At night they would sit in the garden and watch the skies, his father educating him on the different stars, his knowledge seemingly endless, while his mother contented herself with sitting and listening to them.

Hesper was fascinated and asked many questions of his father. He repeatedly told him about the Evening Star, Hesperus, and its position in the sky until he knew it by heart.

Although the house was isolated, his parent's friends in the area constantly visited and stayed for the evening meal which went on long after he was in bed asleep. The one thing he remembered was the permanent supply of food on the table. And if anyone fell on hard times, his mother was the first one to help them out.

Then, one night, shortly after his mother's friend had left, his father had returned unexpectedly. Seeing the man leave, his father had enquired as to who he was. His mother explained that he had been a family friend from before they had married and that he visited from time to time. For the first time that he could remember Hesper heard his parents arguing. He buried his head in the bed and tried to shut it out. Eventually everything went quiet and he heard his father go out into the night. In despair he sobbed until finally he cried himself to sleep, the arguing still playing over in his mind.

The next thing he remembered was waking up and coughing violently. He was instantly aware that the house was on fire. He called to his mother and father in terror but he got no response. Rushing into his parents' room he found his mother lying in bed, asleep. He tried to wake her, unsuccessfully. He also realised that his father had not returned. Thinking that he should find him to help his mother, he rushed to the stairs. In his haste he slipped and fell to the bottom, cracking his head violently on the stone floor.

He awoke to find himself in great pain. He dragged himself across the floor to the door and outside, hoping to see his father but to no avail.

By this time the fire had taken hold and, as he watched, he knew that his mother was dying in the flames. He never found his father.

Over and over he played out different scenarios in his mind as to what had happened, steadfastly avoiding the most evident truth – that his father had burned down the house knowing that both he and his mother were asleep inside it.

As he watched the flames licking into the sky, he whispered to the house "If only we could go back and stop it happening." Instantly he felt an unbelievable pain in his chest. Somehow he knew that his very soul had been taken from him. It had been viscously wrenched from his body.

After the conflagration, after he had regained consciousness, he had attempted to throw himself on the kindness of his neighbours or his parents' friends, but such was the shame of the event, they had all turned their backs on him, refusing to recognise even his existence.

He was reduced to begging on the streets among people who rejected him and treated him as a stranger.

Damn his eyes, he thought to himself, and then, curling up against Merlin for comfort, he sobbed soundlessly to the wind.

Chapter 15

"Did you and Merlin have an enjoyable walk, Hesper?" Shasta asked as he hobbled in. She couldn't help noticing his puffy eyes indicating he had been crying at some point.

"Yes, thank you, Shasta," he answered, very subdued.

Unsure of the situation, she tried again. "Did you go to the beach?"

"No, I went to my old house. I often go there. It helps me to remember my parents."

With a sudden gush of sympathy and understanding she moved towards him to hold him.

At first he stood firm, and then his lower lip began to tremble and he hobbled forward towards her and collapsed in tears in her open arms. Merlin softly meowed sharing the pain.

Shasta held his frail body until the tears subsided, her kind heart feeling desperately sorry for his loss. She resolved there and then that if ever she and Erasmus had a child she would ensure that Hesper never felt neglected and always part of the family.

Finally his tears stopped flowing and, with her help, he lay down in his bed. Lightly covering him, she marvelled at the way Merlin instantly took up his position at Hesper's head.

Inseparable, she thought, and went to sit in the garden. From her favourite seat she watched the sea as the waves slowly ebbed and flowed and wondered what Erasmus was doing at this time. She hadn't seen him for a few days.

After the initial frenzy of discovering love, they had fallen into a pattern of taking time in between meetings. This made their time together even more special.

She was expecting her very close friend Esmeralda to visit tonight, so she sat and awaited her arrival.

When she arrived, Shasta greeted her using the familiar shortened version of her name.

"Hello, Esme, how are you?"

"Yes, I'm well, thank you. I see that love agrees with you, Shasta. You're absolutely glowing."

"I have to admit I have never been happier," she said, smiling.

"How are things now with Hesper? Has he settled in all right with you? I often hear his laughter in the garden when he plays with Merlin. It's a joy to behold when you consider his affliction."

"Actually, dear Esme, I was hoping to ask you about that." She motioned her to a seat. "You used to live quite close to that ruined house on the rocks."

"Yes."

"Did you ever know anybody to live there?"

"No, the house has been a ruin for as long as anybody can remember. Why?"

Shasta frowned. "It is something that Hesper told me. He appears absolutely convinced that his story is true but it cannot be. If it is true, it must have happened many, many years ago."

"But Hesper is but a boy."

"Yes, he is but a boy."

"Why, what does he say?"

"Well, he says that his father was a merchant and quite wealthy. Several times a month he would travel by boat into Cornwall and trade with other merchants. In his absence, his mother took to regularly entertaining a man at their house. He just seemed to appear out of nowhere, almost as if he had stepped off a cloud that was passing. He was a very good looking man, according to Hesper, with a neatly trimmed beard."

Shasta took in a deep breath and checked that Hesper was still sleeping. She needn't have worried because he and Merlin were exactly as she had left them.

Esme, eager to hear more, indicated so.

"Hesper says that his father had been away and returned unexpectedly to find that a man had been visiting the house and had been doing so regularly in his absence. Hesper's mother explained that the man was a friend of long standing. Hesper's father, being of a jealous nature, demanded to know exactly what had been going on. His mother tried to convince him that nothing had happened, but to no avail. Evidently his father stormed out of the house into the night. After that Hesper is uncertain as to what happened. He awoke to find the house on fire and his mother unconscious in his parents' bedroom. Rushing to get help, he fell down the stairs. When he regained consciousness, it was too late. He dragged himself out of the house but his mother perished in the flames and his father was nowhere to be found. When he approached his neighbours, they refused to even recognise his existence."

Shasta looked meaningfully at Esme.

"I remember my parents mentioning the visit of a boy. But he didn't exist. Nobody has lived there for maybe a hundred years. Was that boy Hesper? He could not have come from the house. Whoever he is, he did not come from there."

"Oh well, whoever he is, he is here now," said Shasta contentedly.

"Hesper's story does not concern you?"

Shasta smiled. "No, not at all."

Esme held Shasta's hand earnestly. "You have a good heart, Shasta. Be careful."

"I have indeed been warned," Shasta replied, "but all will turn out well. A beggar boy is now a well fed and contented member of our family".

After Esme had left, Shasta sat and looked out over the ocean. The moon reflected itself onto the sea and sent out sparkling shimmers which seemed to dance across the waves. It reminded her of the first night she had met up with Erasmus. She made up her mind that henceforth Hesper's life would be as comfortable as she could make it. From now on he would get only the best she had to offer.

Chapter 16

Erasmus had been sitting in his cave contemplating his future with Shasta. He had made up his mind to accept Hesper as his adopted son. He had a common interest of astronomy with the boy. At times when he gave lectures and informal talks he had been astounded by the boy's knowledge of the subject. Whilst he had been consulting charts the boy had the information stored in his head. Somehow it didn't bother him that the boy got in first with his answers. In fact at times it was quite amusing for him. Apparently he had been taught by his father over many years. Realistically he knew nothing about the boy except that his given name meant Evening Star. This in itself made him rather special in Erasmus' eyes.

Strange, he thought to himself. Since I became involved with Shasta not once have I thought of home or going back in time. It's as if this is my home and time now.

With this thought, he let out a deep sigh. He was content. Suddenly he felt guilty. Not once had he thought his mother. Well a quick visit wouldn't do any harm.

Sitting quietly he waited to be transported back in time. Nothing happened. Panic set in and he tried again. This time he could see his mother but still he was rooted in the present time. He tried to reach out and touch her. He could see her sitting in her kitchen looking old and frail. How had she aged so quickly, he thought to himself? Have I been away so long?

Again he tried but still nothing happened. As the vision had come, so it went, and he was left looking at the bare wall of the back of the cave.

What had happened, he thought to himself. Am I losing my powers? Is this what love does to you? Does this mean I will never be able to go back again? For a moment he panicked again. What could he do?

Suddenly inspiration struck. He would visit the woman in the market place. What was her name, Lyandra? No it wasn't that. Liana, yes, that was it. She might have the answer. With speed he left the cave and went straight to the market.

As luck would have it she was there, sitting quietly on her own with her eyes closed.

As he approached and without opening her eyes she said "So, Erasmus, you return?

Without even considering the fact that she knew it was him he immediately sat in front of her showing his urgency.

"Liana, I just tried to get back to my own time to make a short visit to my mother and nothing happened. I just couldn't go back. What has happened to me? I have always been in control of my actions. I am omnipotent, Liana!" Frustration made him blurt all this out in one. Normally he would be more self-controlled but no longer.

"No, you're in love, Erasmus. There is a difference."

"What do you mean?" he asked startled and a little bit fearful if he was honest with himself.

"Emotions, Erasmus, emotions. We let our guards down when we are in love and become vulnerable. There is nothing we can do about it. We see things differently and become softer in our feelings and ways. Before you were always in control of your actions, and responsible to no one. Now you have taken on responsibilities in your life and it has changed you into a human being. A rather nice one if I may be permitted to say so. I didn't like the old Erasmus. He was nasty and assumed he was superior to all. Now you have become mortal and it takes some getting used to. Eventually, when you accept things, you will be able to go back to your time but it will be different. You will just have to wait until fate decides the time is right for you. Now go and let an old woman sleep in peace. But remember all is not as it seems."

With that she waved him away. The discussion was at an end as far as she was concerned.

Dejectedly he slowly walked away and back along the beach. He didn't like being so vulnerable. He wasn't used to it. What was happening to him? He loved Shasta to the depths of his soul but he didn't expect to lose his powers in exchange for it. With mixed emotions and a heavy heart he made his way back to his cave. He contemplated going to see Shasta but decided he needed some time on his own to think. He would see her tomorrow . It wasn't as if she was that far away.

Chapter 17

The night had not been easy for Erasmus. He tried again to go back to his own time but again with no success. Once again he could see his mother but not touch her. Finally he had fallen into a fitful sleep of travelling through time and being stranded. He also dreamt of Hesper, seeing him as a fit and healthy man.

Shaking off his fears, he went to see Shasta and they decided to take Hesper to spend the day lazing on the beach. It was taken for granted that Merlin would join them, although he ensured he kept a safe distance from any water.

It gave Erasmus the chance to voice his fears to Shasta and also enlighten her on his visit to Liana. She finally admitted to him that she had seen danger for him when she read the tea leaves in his cup at the lecture.

Shasta just had to ask the question. "Would you be very unhappy if you couldn't go back to your own time Erasmus?" she asked, secretly dreading the answer.

He looked long and hard at her as if weighing up the answer. "Yes and no. Yes, because I can only see my mother in a vision. No, because you have now become my life and I never want to be parted from you. I have had many women in my life, Shasta, I don't deny that, but I never realised how love can make you feel inside. I love you with my whole heart and soul."

"Oh Erasmus," was all she could say, completely overwhelmed by his admissions of love and at the same time completely accepting his admissions of other women. He was a good looking man and she supposed it was to be expected.

To a certain extent he seemed to accept the lessening of his powers. If it was a choice between his power and losing Shasta there would be no contest. Shasta would win every time. In the meantime he put it to the back of his mind and enjoyed the rest of the day. If it were in his power he would make Hesper whole again as shown in his dream. But watching the speed he got around he wondered if it would be a good thing after all.

As he watched Hesper, he was also aware that he was being watched in turn by the boy. It was a strange look, thought Erasmus, almost hostile at times, but he couldn't think why and put it down to his imagination.

Later that evening he sat quietly in the garden at Shasta's house. The three of them had had their fill of good food. Shasta sat beside him as they watched Hesper and Merlin playing with the mouse on the stick that he had bought. Hesper rarely wore the shirt he had purchased but tonight he had deigned to wear it.

He felt at peace with the world as he watched the sun set on the horizon and then the moon taking its place. From time to time Hesper stopped playing and they discussed different stars that suddenly appeared in the heavens. He knew complete happiness and was content in his new family environment.

Shasta, without his realising it, had shown him humility and he had responded.

Whatever lay in the future he would take it as it came. If there was a danger to be confronted somehow he would deal with it.

Chapter 18

Several time a week Shasta went to the market. It was nice to be out and about and meet up with friends, and look at what new wares were on display. Hesper usually accompanied her along with Merlin who only just fitted into the basket these days. Both of them seemed to be growing daily and most of her trips were to top up her cupboard which seemed constantly half full. Although Erasmus ate with them regularly, he didn't seem to eat as much as Hesper. They laughed it off as Hesper being a growing boy.

Hesper surprised her the most. He rarely used his crutch these days and somehow he seemed to be getting about better on his leg, which seemed to be filling out and getting stronger. At first she put it down to her imagination and then to the nourishing food he was being fed daily. Hesper, at these suggestions, just smiled and agreed. Merlin, they concurred, was definitely getting fatter. Very soon, she decided, he would have to walk to the market or stay at home as he was becoming too heavy to carry around.

Today he was happily walking along beside Hesper, rarely straying more than a couple of feet in front him. Occasionally Hesper picked him up if there were too many people about and he seemed content to sit around the back of his neck, much to the amusement of passersby.

Liana was in her usual place and, leaving Hesper to roam at will for a while, Shasta decided to wait her turn to speak to her. It was quite pleasant sitting in the late autumn sunshine. Best to make the most of it, she thought. Before so long, winter will set in.

Almost as if in answer, a distant rumbling could be heard out to sea. Looks like we may be in for some rain then, she thought to herself. Heaven knows, the garden could do with it after the scorching summer we've had.

"Did you want to talk to me, Shasta?" asked Liana suddenly breaking into her thoughts unexpectedly.

Goodness she was miles away thinking of all sorts.

Moving forward she greeted Liana and posed her question carefully. "Erasmus has been trying for some time to revisit his own time unsuccessfully. Why is this, Liana?"

"Erasmus is in love"

"I don't understand, Liana. How does that effect his movement through time?"

"By being in love with you he has become more emotional. This makes him more vulnerable and consequently it takes away his strength of resolve. Perhaps he doesn't want to return to his own time, my dear. Maybe he is content where he is, therefore his subconscious won't let him go. Erasmus is not used to weakness of any kind and finds it difficult to cope with."

While Shasta was taking this in, Liana said "Hesper seems to be improving in health, I see. You are certainly making a man of him."

"I love him dearly, Liana. When Erasmus and I are wed, we will accept and love him as our own son. Erasmus has grown equally fond of him."

"Heed my warning Shasta. All is not as it seems. Now go!"

With that she was dismissed, unable to question further.

As always, Shasta came away from Liana with even more unanswered questions than when she started out. She made up her mind not to approach Liana again, but deep in her heart she knew that she would of course.

Chapter 19

"Yes, that's it. I've got it!" shouted Erasmus to anyone who was listening outside of his cave that morning.

Tripping over his own feet in his haste, he stumbled and fell on to the sand. Laughing, he got up and carried on towards Shasta's house, only to feel disappointment on discovering she wasn't there. She must be in the market place, he thought, and made off there. He passed several people on the way who remarked on the change in him of late. He was no longer the strange caveman, as he had become known locally.

Finally he caught sight of her in the distance and hurried to catch up. As he called her name she turned and hurried back to meet him. With eyes for only each other, neither saw the look of annoyance on Hesper's face or Merlin digging his claws in the back of his neck.

He explained his idea and wondered how she felt about it. Her face lit up.

"That would be wonderful, Erasmus, but you would need a lot of help."

"Well I'm sure the neighbours will help. After all, I have helped them often enough. If we do it at night mostly, he won't really know. We will need to hurry though as the seasons are against us."

Putting his plan to the neighbours, they were only too glad to help out and agreed much haste was needed if they were to be finished before the weather got too bad.

So for the next couple of months Erasmus worked solidly on the project. From the front nothing looked very different but at the back it was a different matter. Everything started to take shape.

Shasta was content to see him when she could and Hesper seemed quite content with things as they were also. So the pattern was set. Finally on a very cold mid December morning, it was finished. The women had lent a hand where necessary, and Erasmus could hardly contain himself. He felt wonderful looking at all he had achieved. He reminisced on his former years when he had considered himself so superior to everyone. This feeling of self-satisfaction was far better.

Whistling to himself he walked to Shasta's house. She was overjoyed to hear the news and decided that they should keep quiet about it until after the evening meal. For now it would be their secret.

Explaining to Hesper that they would be eating early this evening, and putting off her friend Esme until the following evening, they sat down to eat.

Erasmus and Shasta couldn't eat their food fast enough. When it was finally finished, they told Hesper what had been done.

He looked aghast and went ashen. Then his face went bright red with anger.

"You have rebuilt my parent's house? Without even asking how I felt about it? Did you not even consider that I would like to be consulted?"

Erasmus and Shasta looked on in astonishment, firstly because of his outburst, but mostly because his persona seemed to change in stature. His body looked larger and stronger and his eyes went from blue to black.

Instantly, and in turn, the old Erasmus was back. His eyes went from blue placid pools to black coals. Pulling his body to its full height he said "How dare you, you ungrateful little wretch? Have you any idea how much hard work went into rebuilding that house, the amount of people that have helped simply because they wanted to make amends to you for their neglect of you in the past? There have been days when our hands have bled and our backs virtually broken, and you question why we did it?"

Taken back and surprised by Erasmus' reaction, Hesper immediately reverted to the little boy again. "I'm sorry, Erasmus, please forgive me. It was such a shock. Will you take me to see it?"

Instantly Erasmus quietened down. "Perhaps I should apologise too. I thought you would be pleased. I know you often visit the ruin and I felt it would be nice to see it rebuilt."

Shasta sat down, getting her breath back. She couldn't believe the difference in both of them. With Hesper, it was because of the change in him. Suddenly, it seemed like she was watching and listening to a mature man. Erasmus, she had never seen lose his temper so she was equally shocked at the way he raged at the boy.

Thank goodness for the calm which had now settled. Even Merlin had retreated to the basket. He was far too big for it now but still he tried to curl up in it out of harm's way.

Now that they were both calm, Erasmus agreed to walk to the house with Hesper. Shasta decided to stay with Merlin. It wasn't a very pleasant evening and she preferred to stay in the warm by the fire. In the distance she could hear the sea roaring as it crashed against the shore. Besides it would give them time to get over their differences, she thought to herself.

Looking back, she realised that she hadn't noticed how much Hesper had matured since he had been with her. It seemed that Erasmus had mellowed as time went on and Hesper now showed signs of aggression. A couple of times before he had reacted similarly, but she had put that down to the frustration of his leg. No excuses now, though, she thought. There had been a dramatic improvement. He never used his crutch and, apart from a slight limp when he was tired, no one would ever recognise him as the boy he was. The leg had filled out and now looked no different to the other one. Thinking about it, his body had really filled out as well. Why hadn't she noticed the changes in his body before? In the heat of the summer he had barely worn clothes at all apart from breeches and, yes, his shirts did now look a bit tight. She really had to consider buying him some more. She would see to it tomorrow at the market.

Chapter 20

As Erasmus and Hesper made their way towards the house, the strong wind beat them back. With their heads down there wasn't much chance of talking or voicing their opinions on their recent outburst.

Hesper, for his part, had regretted it bitterly. He had shown his other self far sooner than he intended. He would have to learn more self control. His time was not yet. A few more weeks and he would be ready.

Erasmus walked silently to the house. He recalled all of the hard work that had been put into it. Many nights he had gone back to his cave his back breaking from his toil. He had not even considered food; he had been too tired. Many hours had been put in also by the friends helping him. Yes, he considered them friends now and had begun to feel like part of the community. They had all worked together, stone by back-breaking stone, in atrocious weather sometimes; then that boy asked how we dared build without consulting him.

It still angered him to the core of his soul but he also had to recognise that he hadn't consulted Hesper who claimed it to be his home, although he had never explained how or why. Erasmus and Shasta had even speculated that Hesper might be a time traveller too, projected forward by a tragedy, who had got stuck here in this time, as Erasmus had. If only he would admit it. Why such secrecy?

Whatever the explanation, Erasmus had thought Hesper would have been so pleased with the surprise. Well, time would tell. They were nearly there.

They both started to walk with more earnest as if in silent agreement. Finally, with red faces and watery eyes from the high wind, they arrived.

From a distance, the front still looked derelict but, close up, Hesper could see the improvements that had been made and the all round appearance. He admitted to himself that a lot of hard work had been put into it and he should be grateful to Erasmus. But he wasn't prepared to admit to that just yet. He wanted to see inside first.

As he walked round to the side of the house and inside, he stopped. It looked exactly as it had done before the fire. Even the garden area had been tended.

"It probably looks nothing like the way you remember it," Erasmus ventured.

"It looks exactly the way I remember it."

Erasmus frowned. How could that be? Was the boy telling the truth or merely humouring him.

Hesper knew exactly how that could be.

As Erasmus stood back and watched, he could see the boy suddenly become smaller in stature. His shoulders hunched and his body shook with emotion. As he moved forward to console him he shook him off. Wiping the tears with the back of his hand he recovered himself instantly.

"Yes, well, I suppose I need to thank you for your part in this. Can we go now? I'm tired."

Realising that the boy was overcome but trying hard to hide it, he agreed that they should get back and maybe visit again tomorrow in daylight. As they left the house, a seagull swooped over the head of Erasmus from the roof, screeching loudly, taking him completely by surprise and causing him to duck down.

Hesper chuckled to himself and moved off the craggy rock back down the hill to Shasta's house, their return journey that much quicker with the wind behind them.

Shasta was eager to hear all about the house she had visited many times but had not seen completed. She intended to go there during the daytime to enable her to have a good look round. Hesper said it was almost identical to the original, which puzzled her, because if that were the case, why was his mood so subdued? Feigning tiredness from the walk, he asked to go to his bed and, disappointed by his lack of enthusiasm, she agreed.

Erasmus, with mixed feelings, had decided to go back to his cave, arranging to see Shasta the following morning. They both intended to look at the house again in daylight.

Over the next few weeks Hesper visited the house often, getting the feel of it again. He seemed reluctant to let anyone else go there. It had been furnished almost the same as before with only a few changes.

It was his. Erasmus had made that quite clear to him. He could come and go as he pleased or stay there permanently if he wished. He had mixed feelings about this as he enjoyed the company of Shasta who had taken him into her home when he was at his lowest ebb. The added bonus to that, of course, was finding Merlin again.

So he spent some of the time in his new home and other times with Shasta. This seemed to work out quite well as Erasmus and Shasta planned to wed soon.

Well, we will see what happens after that, he thought to himself, and he let out a heinous laugh which no one but he and the seagull on top of his roof heard.

Chapter 21

Christmas came and went, celebrated by the three of them at Shasta's house. Much food was eaten and presents exchanged. Many friends were visited and they in return called on Shasta and Erasmus to continue the celebrations. In the New Year Hesper decided he wanted to spend more time in his own home which he did with their blessing.

As the cold winter came to an end, the wedding of Erasmus and Shasta drew near.

It had been delayed until the early spring for several reasons. Now, as the spring sunshine did its best to warm the earth, the area took on a new life. Local people began to come out and about, taking walks along the beach eager to rid themselves of the winter cobwebs. Although there wasn't much warmth in the sun, there was a promise of warmth to come.

Hespers' leg was hardly noticeable now. No one had any answer for it but just regarded it as a gift of fate to be accepted without question.

Erasmus, in his quieter moments, had tried several times to return to his own time with no success. As he sat in his cave, he had many visions but had to accept that he could now only watch his mother from afar. Occasionally he saw his sisters. Their families still seemed to increase yearly but he was sad to see his mother looking so frail.

Maybe this was the price he had to pay for true love, he thought.

Shasta sympathised with him, but she had convinced herself that if he was able to travel back to his own time she would never see him again. She would be devastated if he went and then couldn't return. The sooner they were wed the better.

Shasta had decided on a small ceremony in the local church near the market. Her dress was being made for her by Esme and she would have a head-dress and bouquet of spring flowers. Hesper would wear black breeches, black shoes, long white socks and a white silk shirt. This was much to his disgust but he agreed to it to please her. He was now as tall as Erasmus and, although slimmer, he was certainly sturdy.

Merlin would wear a white silk ribbon so as not to be left out. It was now just a matter of the day arriving.

Shasta had gone to visit Esme to finalise fittings of the dress and Erasmus decided to visit Hesper. He hadn't seen him for nearly two weeks and he wanted to reassure himself that he was alright. He was convinced that they had done the right thing in rebuilding the house. Hesper had settled in well and was enjoying his independence, safe in the knowledge of being able to visit Shasta if he got fed up with his own company.

As he now approached the house, the first thing he noticed was the seagull on the roof. It seemed to have taken an intense dislike to him. Every time he visited the house, the bird dived at him. On one occasion he had actually pecked the top of his head. Hesper seemed to find it rather amusing. To a certain extent so did he, but enough was enough.

Yet again, as he approached, the bird was there watching. He had to admit it was one of the largest he had seen. He felt a bit foolish hurrying to take cover from a bird but he did so anyway, calling out to Hesper as he approached the door. It swung open unexpectedly, casting dark shadows around the room. Hesper was sitting in a chair in the far corner in the shadows, hardly visible. His body was completely ramrod straight and his head held high. He was at home in his own little kingdom. By his side was his faithful Merlin. How had he got here, Erasmus thought? He certainly hadn't noticed him on the way up here.

Erasmus, for the first time in his life, felt a strange feeling of fear and yet this was a young boy and a cat. At the same time he felt his energy being drained from him. Nothing like this had happened to him before. He felt weak around his knees as if his legs wouldn't support him.

"Are you alright, Erasmus?" Hesper asked with concern in his voice. "Would you like to sit down and have a drink?"

"I do feel a bit tired" he said.

Trying not to make too much of a fuss, Erasmus made his way to the nearest chair, somehow reluctant to admit how he felt. Hopefully, if he stayed still for a while he would feel better.

Up until this moment Hesper hadn't stirred. Now he moved with cat-like grace to get Erasmus a drink. As he watched him, Erasmus realised he was no longer looking at a young boy. The change in him was amazing and he had to admit to himself that he hadn't really noticed.

He only had sisters, and basically had been a loner in his pubescent years. He was aware of his own good looks but just accepted bodily changes as they occurred.

Still unsure of his own feeling of weakness, he decided to concentrate on that, gingerly moving his legs about to keep the feeling going.

As Hesper handed him a drink and returned to his chair, the room suddenly became incredibly dark. Hesper seemed to be surrounded by dark shadows which made him seem menacing. Through the open door he could see the sky in the distance rapidly turning black. As he looked back into the room again he noticed that Merlin was now seated in the middle of Hesper's lap and also watching him from the shadows.

"It looks like we are in for a storm, Erasmus. You can stay here if you like and eat with me. That way you can ride out the storm. Or, if you prefer to leave shortly, you should be back with Shasta before it starts."

Erasmus was starting to feel strangely uncomfortable in Hesper's presence, so he decided to return to Shasta.

Bidding Hesper farewell, he thanked him for the drink and left. He was relieved to note that the seagull had disappeared for once.

As he walked away from the craggy rock, he began to feel better and stronger in himself. Perhaps I just needed the fresh air, he though to himself, and, as he reached Shasta's house, the first large drops of rain began to fall before the storm set in. There would be many more before summer arrived.

Hesper hadn't moved and Merlin was still seated on his lap as before. Slowly the flames parted and he saw a vision of Erasmus and Shasta sitting beside their own fire.

"Very soon, Erasmus," he said to his four walls, "very soon," letting out a heinous cackle as the seagull flew in and settled on the table.

Chapter 22

Finally, the day of the wedding arrived and the morning was superb. The sun competed with fluffy white clouds and won. It was by no means hot but at least it was warm.

Erasmus was told to go to the church with Hesper and was not allowed to see Shasta until she arrived there. Merlin was confined to the house more or less, but he spent most of his time at Hesper's house these days anyway.

Esme had arrived to help Shasta prepare. Whilst they dressed they both discussed the prospects of the coming nuptials. Shasta was so excited her fingers were all thumbs and eventually she left it to Esme to help her to get into her dress which was a fine print of delicate flowers. As she placed her arms in the dress, it sensuously flowed over the shape of her slim body. Finally Esme placed the delicate head-dress, on the crown of her head. The hair, which had been left loose and flowing, had been brushed until it shone.

She was ready.

They had decided to do away with tradition as it was such a beautiful day and walked to the church. This was much to the amusement of everyone they met on the way. Shasta looked beautiful and was very popular.

As she passed by people, she was constantly asking them to join her in the church and eventually she had quite a procession behind her. This was her day and she could do nothing but smile at her good fortune in meeting Erasmus.

When they were wed they would be the perfect family even if Hesper were staying at his own house. She had already begun looking on him as her son.

The wedding went without a hitch and hand in hand they walked back to the house where a feast had been prepared by neighbours during their ceremony.

There was much ribald laughter and many glasses of ale were drunk by all. Shasta and Erasmus couldn't have been happier if they had been given all the stars in the heavens as a present.

Prior to the wedding Erasmus still considered the cave his home as he had everything he required there. Now that he and Shasta were together the cave became more of a workplace. He was still reluctant to have any visitors there and his privacy there was respected by all.

Life set into an idyllic pattern for both of them. They entertained neighbours and friends and in turn were entertained also.

Hesper seemed content to spend most of his time in his own house, almost recluse-like, but at the same time recognising that Erasmus and Shasta still looked on him as a son. He had changed several things in the interior rooms of late which, although to his liking, surprised Shasta and Erasmus. It gave the house a feeling of isolation rather than warmth, but they recognised that it suited him.

Shasta often remarked that if she didn't know better, she would have thought that he wasn't living alone, judging by the plates in the sink.

On one occasion Shasta took a basket of food for him and Merlin. As she approached the door she heard voices coming from inside. She recognised Hesper's voice, but the second voice was very masculine and deep. Knocking loudly she opened the door and then called out. On entering the room it was only occupied by Hesper who was sitting reading a book. She thought it felt cold in the room and pulled her shawl tighter.

"Hello, Shasta, you look confused. Is anything wrong?"

"When I came to the door I'm sure I heard voices. I thought you had a visitor."

"No, there is only me here. Perhaps you heard me reading aloud."

"Oh yes, of course," she said unconvinced.

The voice was far too deep to have been his.

"I've brought you some provisions from the market, Hesper. I thought it easier if I brought them up to you now rather than you have to bring them back after your meal with us tonight. You haven't forgotten have you? Erasmus is looking forward to it especially now that the nights are warmer. We thought maybe we could sit in the garden afterwards or go for a walk along the beach. What do you think?"

"Well maybe not the beach, but it will be nice to sit in the garden again. We haven't done that for a long time."

"Very well, Hesper, we will expect you at the usual time then."

As she left she was convinced that she could hear voices again. She didn't use her physic ability very much these days but she felt sure there was someone there. Also there seemed to be a faint smell of smoke in the house and yet no fire was lit.

Looking to the roof of the house she half expected to see smoke rising from the smoke stack, but there was only the seagull which Erasmus had told her about. She smiled to herself. He looked harmless enough just sitting there.

Clearing her mind she walked back to her own house enjoying the salty taste of the sea on her lips.

After their dinner she and Erasmus regularly walked along the beach in the moonlight. Sitting on her favourite rock they watched Hesperus the Evening Star appear and then, one by one, the other stars joined in. She had hoped Hesper would be there tonight. There was something urgent and joyful she wished to convey to Erasmus and Hesper at the same time, the news that she was with child.

Although Hesper already knew.

Chapter 23

The meal with Hesper was not at all successful. He seemed to pick arguments with Erasmus the whole evening. It began during dinner and continued as they sat in the garden.

Shasta had decided to keep her own counsel. They both knew far more than she did on the subject. Admittedly Hesper's knowledge of astronomy was now equal to Erasmus', and frequently, if charts were to be drawn up, preference was given to Hesper over Erasmus. Erasmus didn't seemed particularly put out by this as he regarded the boy as his own son anyway. He was content with his life with Shasta, and astronomy and charts were now taking second place. However in Erasmus's mind he was still far more knowledgeable and so they would agree to disagree by the end of the evening.

It was agreed, though, that Erasmus would collect up all of his charts of the various constellations and bring them to Hesper's house the following evening. They would spend the evening studying them. If it got too late, Erasmus would stay the night.

As Erasmus made his way up to the rocky crag, he felt there was a hint of rain in the air. All day it had been threatening and he got the feeling that there would be a storm before the night was out. Well, if it happened, he would spend the night with Hesper as arranged.

As he neared the house, he noticed that the seagull wasn't there. Perhaps he didn't know I was coming tonight, he thought to himself and laughed.

Reaching the door he called out and walked in as usual. Hesper was sitting in his chair waiting expectantly. He had a strange, almost serene, expression on his face.

"Hello, Father."

Erasmus stood completely still. It was such a normal statement to make but, coming from Hesperus, it was........well he wasn't sure. He was surprised, flattered even. Hesper had only ever called him Erasmus. Many times he had asked him if he would like to refer to him as his father but Hesper had remained steadfast. So Erasmus had accepted it.

This had been a spontaneous remark, said with some degree of warmth, but the eyes looked cold and defiant.

Erasmus had noticed this before but assumed it was just something that came along with puberty. However the words were said and he hoped to improve their relationship tonight. This was one of his prime reasons for being here.

Hesper offered him a drink and they cleared the table ready to place out all the charts they had.

For a while they seemed to get along amicably enough and then Hesper challenged something Erasmus had drawn on the chart. Knowing he was right, Erasmus argued the point fiercely. The discussion got more and more heated.

Suddenly the threatened storm broke and rain began to beat down mercilessly as if to add weight to the argument which had now developed.

"You cannot be right, Father," said Hesper suddenly calming down. Erasmus looked at him.

"Why do you suddenly refer to me as 'Father', Hesper?" said Erasmus also changing tact.

Out of the corner of his eye Erasmus caught sight of Merlin sitting in the corner of the room watching the exchange.

"You are my father, Erasmus, and I can prove it."

Fortunately there was a chair close to Erasmus. He sank into it. First he looked astonished and then started to laugh until his sides were fit to burst.

All the while Hesper stood his ground. He was now standing over Erasmus, his hands grasping the sides of the chair. As Erasmus stopped laughing and looked into his eyes once again he felt fear. The boy seemed to have grown out of all proportion. His voice now seemed to roar. Erasmus started to feel weak again and in need of air. The room suddenly closed in on him and his head began to swim.

"How am I your father, Hesper?"

"You are my father; Shasta is my mother."

Erasmus was stupefied. "Your mother? How can she be your mother?"

"You will kill us, your wife and your son. You love us, yet you will set fire to our house, this very house, out of jealousy while we sleep, and you will leave us to die. You will do it. You have done it. You will not do it again."

Hesper stood watching him for a few moments and then he drew himself up to his full height, towering over Erasmus.

"I can prove I'm your son, Erasmus," he said and, turning, he indicated the small blemish at the base of his spine that he had been born with. His mother had called it his little star.

"I know that it's identical to yours because I have seen it when you have been bathing. I always ensured that mine was covered at all times. As for time travel, yes, we can both time travel. I am your son, remember? You have travelled from the past. I have travelled from the future which is the past."

Suddenly there was an almighty crack of thunder which brought him back to the present. The rain was still beating down on the roof relentlessly.

Hesper roared out loud "You were born by the storm and now you will die by the storm, Erasmus."

Erasmus felt the colour drain from his face. He tried to leave but felt powerless to do so. His whole body felt weak. Somewhere in the recess of his mind he realised that Hesper was draining the life from him.

"There will be no point in you fighting me, Erasmus. I have been slowly draining your energy for weeks. That's why you are unable to time travel anymore. Now you know why my body healed and, yes, your friends were right, it can only be put down to fate. Your energy is the only thing that I want from you now that you have given my mother a child and I shall be reborn. You will not have the chance to destroy us again."

As he grew weaker, Erasmus screamed ".... No....!", but it was carried away by the storm.

Hesper scooped up Merlin in his arms and shouted for the heavens to hear "I am Hesperus, the omnipotent one," and with that he disappeared before Erasmus's eyes.

Erasmus screamed out the name of his beloved Shasta and fell to the floor.

Chapter 24

Shasta loved to walk along the beach under the stars she had so many times wished upon. Now, kneeling against the rock, the tears streamed down her face as she held the limp form of her beloved Erasmus.

She had found him here when she had gone to search for him. How he had got here she would never know. She tried to understand what he was saying but could only make out that he had been trying to get back to Hesper, his son. His head was cradled in her arms and his breath was coming in short gasps. She would never know.

As she held him in her arms his human form began suddenly to change. Starting with his lower limbs, he became a slithering mass of rotating fluid-like substance, which began to blend with the algae and rocks.

Here he would stay protected by the elements until in another time a young girl would once again unleash the vortex that would forever be Erasmus the Omnipotent.

Made in the USA
Charleston, SC
20 November 2011